D1320595

THE
OWL

A Story for Children

□

WRITTEN BY

DAVID MAMET
& LINDSAY CROUSE

ILLUSTRATED BY

STEPHEN ALCORN

□

THE KIPLING PRESS
NEW YORK

 A GOBLIN TALE

Text copyright © 1987 by David Mamet and
Lindsay Crouse
Art copyright © 1987 by Stephen Alcorn
Printed in the U.S.A. All rights reserved. Distributed to
the trade by Kampmann & Co.
Designed by Wendy Palitz.
ISBN 0-943718-01-5
The Kipling Press
First Edition

THE
OWL

Steven had lain down on the couch to rest. It was the last day of the month, and the air had turned cold. All afternoon he'd worked outside. There was a pile of old lumber back behind the barn. It had been there from the time they tore down the well house, lying beneath some rusted, corrugated roofing sheets.

All afternoon Steven moved the lumber inside the barn, and worked at pulling out the nails, at sorting the pieces. He

checked his plans and arranged the pieces of wood; then he constructed a snug little house for his ducks. He meant to keep them safe inside the barn, warm through the winter. The poultry house was of his own design.

He'd raised the ducks from day-old chicks. His father had bought them for him at the feed store. They were his pets. Over the summer, he'd come to call each of them by name. One of the females had a blue ribbon tied around her neck.

As fall came on, he saw that his choices were to let the ducks go to fly South, or to keep them warm all winter in the barn. The second choice entailed the greater work, since he would have to feed and water them and muck out their house every day. He could let them go, but the books said that they would not stand a good chance of making the long flight south. They had been raised in a pen and were unused to the wild. So the boy planned the duck house and found the lumber. He had kept the project a surprise, to show his father after it was done. Tomorrow, he would move the ducks from their outside run to their new home in the barn.

He had not seen his ducks since morning. It was time to feed them. He went inside to wash up and to put dinner on

the stove before his father got back from town.

He was tired from the work and from the cold, and he sat to rest for one moment on his bed.

Above the bed was the calendar. This month's picture was of two ducks on a pond. The boy looked at it and smiled. Then he lay down in his bed.

He was asleep when he heard the owl scream. He sat up in bed, breathing fast. In his dream it sounded as if the owl was in his room, and he was frightened.

The boy yelled for his father. He ran out of the room and down the stairs. He looked out the living room window, searching for his father in the yard. He saw that his ducks were running, flapping their wings, trying to get into the air. Above them was an owl, just gone into its swoop, falling on the ducks to kill them. He flung open the window. He screamed at the owl; the owl stopped its swoop and beat the air to gain altitude.

Steven ran through the kitchen and out the back door. He saw the ducks as they scattered. They were running for the shelter of the barn, the porch, the tall grass, anything that might protect them from the owl's next swoop. The duck with the blue ribbon screeched and ran the length of the farmyard looking for escape. The owl once again went into its swoop.

The boy bent down and picked up stones and threw them. He screamed at the owl again. As he screamed his father drove up from the main road in the pickup and stopped by the barn. The boy ran to him.

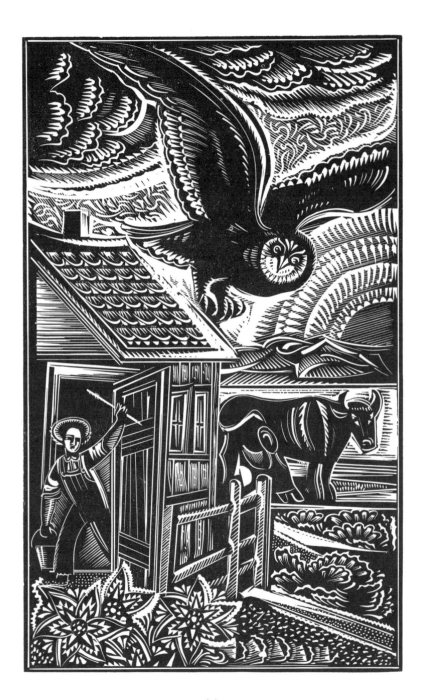

"Get your shotgun," Steven yelled. "Get the gun!"

His father grabbed him by the shoulders. "What is it?"

"The owl."

"What owl?"

"The *owl*, don't you *hear* me?" the boy said. "Go and get your *gun...*"

"What *is* it?" his father said.

"The *owl* is after the *ducks*," Steven said.

"What ducks?"

"The *ducks...my ducks...*"

The boy stopped and tried to catch his breath. His father stepped back and looked at him.

"I was asleep," the boy said. "I was asleep in my room. I heard the owl scream. I woke up..." The boy stopped to breathe again.

"I was frightened. I ran out to you...then I saw him outside. Diving on them..."

"Saw who?" his father said.

"The owl."

"Diving on who?"

Steven paused. "I saw the owl was diving on my ducks..." Steven looked at his father and saw he was very angry. "What is it?" he said.

His father looked at the ground for a long moment. Then he looked up. "Well, I just don't know what to do with you," he said. The man started to walk away. Steven went after him. His father shook his head. "I *told* you not to make a pet of those ducks," he said.

"Will you...will you help me gather them?" Steven said.

"Now stop it, Steven," the man said. "You know they aren't here."

"Of *course* they're here, I just saw them."

"Well, if you're doing this to vex me," the man said, "you're doing just fine. Now you go to your room and think about this."

"But, but," Steven said, "I have to..."

"You know those ducks are gone," the man said. "I've just taken them to the poulterer. They're *gone*, and that's the *end* to it, and I don't see why we have to be foolish about it."

"They're *gone*...?" Steven said.

"And the next time you invent some silly story..." the man said, "an owl does not fly in the day. Now you go to your room."

"I saw the ducks fly," the boy said.

"The ducks are gone. You did not see them fly."

The boy stopped. "They were mine," he said.

His father said nothing.

"They were mine," he said again.

"They belonged to the farm."

"NO," the boy said. "You said that they were *mine*."

"Yes, that is correct," his father said. "They were yours to raise."

The man dug in his pocket and pulled out several dollar bills wrapped in a receipt, and handed the bundle to the boy. The boy opened the receipt. It said, "Burke's Poulterers, The Mountain Road, paid, for 8 ducks, $22. The boy stared at the money.

"There it is," the man said. "Now if you want to apologize, we'll call it quits."

"Apologize for what?" the boy said. "You've sold my...you've sold my ducks."

"Apologize for lying," his father said. The boy stood there; he hung his head. His father looked at him.

"All right," his father said. "When you've changed your mind, you know where I'll be." And the man walked away.

Steven went to his room. Above his bed he saw the calendar with this month's picture of the ducks.

He looked at the picture: the brown female and the green-and-blue headed male. He stopped and stared. There was something in the picture that had not been there before. A spot of color in the background of the print, a smudge of brown. The boy looked and saw it was an owl, in the background, menacing the birds.

He ran out of the room and downstairs.

He stood in the kitchen, his heart beating. He'd come down to call for his father, but how could he? He stood in the

middle of the kitchen floor trying to catch his breath.

There was a huge "thwack," as something hit the kitchen window. He raised his head and saw the large beating wing of the owl. The owl flew off. The boy looked after the owl. The owl rose into the air and dove. It beat its wings to stop the dive, swooped, and perched on the seat of the boy's bicycle, which was leaning against a fence across the yard. The owl stared at the boy. The boy looked at the owl and, slowly, moved to the back door.

He opened the door and stepped into the yard. He leaned forward, as if trying to hear what the bird wanted to say. The owl rose into the air and flew off down the road. It flew back and circled the boy, and flew down the road again. The boy reached in his pocket and took out the bills and the receipt. He looked at the receipt, "Burke's Poulterers, The Mountain Road." Then he got on his bicycle and started down the road.

The poulterer's sign was hanging from the mailbox by the road. The lettering was dark red on white, and the white was dirty.

The boy pedalled up the drive and saw an old farm-house. The house was attached to the barn by a covered walkway. The boy stepped through the walkway and there were his ducks.

The ducks were cramped in a wooden crate, the eight of them in a space no more than six inches high and one and one-half feet on a side. He saw the end of a filthy blue ribbon trailing from the crate. He heard the ducks' wings beating in the confined space. He started toward the crate and heard a voice behind him:

"What do you want?"

He turned around to a man over six feet tall, with huge shoulders and a wild, unshaven face. The man wore rubber hip boots and a white cloth apron, both covered with fresh and drying blood.

The boy was terrified. He wanted to lie; he wanted to calm the man. But he thought of his mission, and he stood up straighter and said:

"I've come for my ducks."

"Which ducks are those?" the man asked.

"These ducks here," Steven said, and he pointed to the wooden crate.

"Well, it seems that you're mistaken," the man said. "I *bought* those ducks two hours ago."

"I know," the boy said. He took out the money and the receipt, "I want to buy them back."

"All right," the man said, staring at the boy. "Eight ducks. Thirty-six dollars."

"You didn't pay anywhere near that much for them," the boy said.

"Not what I paid for 'em. What I *get* for 'em," the man said. "Why don't you go home."

"I'll take them now and pay you later."

"I don't think so," the man said.

"I swear I'll pay you," the boy said.

The man looked at Steven and he said, "Go home. Whatever it is, just go home. I have work to do. These ducks

die tomorrow and that's the end of it." He bent down and picked up Steven's crate of ducks and carried it toward the barn. Over his shoulder he called back, "And don't get foolish with me, boy. These are my property."

Steven waited until the man had gone back into the barn. The night was coming on fast, and it was a long way home. He saw a low shed to one side. He went into the shed.

The place was terrible and dark. It looked like it exuded dark, like blood was seeping out of it. The boy hid in the shed, in the smell of cold blood. He looked between the battens at the barn, until he saw the man leave the barn and walk to his house. He waited for the lights in the house to go out, to show the man had gone to sleep. Steven huddled in his short jacket and drew his hand into the sleeves. He turned the collar up. He wished he had brought his long coat.

When he woke in the dark he was frightened. He was cold; he was in a strange place, and the air smelled of dirt and blood.

He took a deep breath, and after a few minutes his eyes began to get accustomed to the dark. He walked out of the shed and crept across the yard and into the barn. He walked past the bloody band saw where he'd seen the poulterer dismembering the birds. He moved through the darkened

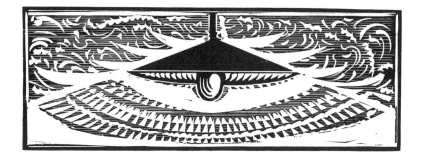

barn. He felt his way along the wall until he came to the door to the killing room. He lifted the cold iron latch.

The room was even darker than the shed. The boy could barely make out the shapes of the crates along the floor. He wondered how he would find his birds.

Feeling his way along the wall, his hand touched a light switch. "I'll flick it on for an instant," he thought. So much light after so much dark blinded him. His eyes hurt terribly. He flicked off the light, but his eyes retained an image of the killing room. Large knives and cleavers hung on the wall. Tables were piled with parts of bird carcasses. Crates were everywhere on the floor. On one, a strange shape was perched and it turned its head to look at the boy. It was the owl. Steven's eyes retained an image of the crate before him with the owl on it.

He kept his eyes squeezed shut and inched forward on

his hands and knees until his hand touched a crate. He slipped off the wire loop that held the lid closed and put his hands inside.

Inside the case he felt the warm birds. He felt his "pet" with the blue ribbon on her neck. He'd found the ducks.

The crate was heavy. He dragged it as quietly as he could out of the killing room. It bumped as he pulled it over the doorstep, and he stopped and listened to see if he had been heard. In the quiet he heard his ducks making soft noises inside the crate. He dragged the crate to the large,

sliding barn door. He pulled the big door open, and the unoiled rollers made a loud shriek in the night.

He heaved the crate outside and opened it. A light went on in the house.

Steven threw the ducks out of the crate as the door to the house opened and the poulterer came out. The man held a shotgun in his hands. "Who is there?" he called. He flipped a switch and the whole barnyard was bathed in light. The man looked at the boy standing by the ducks. "What do you think you're doing?" he said.

The boy yelled at the ducks, "Get *out* of here!" He shooed them, and they began to run and fly away from him. "Go on," he screamed at them, "go *on*!!!"

"What in . . . what do you think you're doing?" the man shouted, and he started toward the boy. Steven backed away.

"Come *back* here," the man said. He pointed the shotgun in the air and touched off one barrel. He stepped between Steve and the path to the main road. The boy looked around, seeking safety. The man started toward him, and the boy began to run into the woods. He heard the man running behind him.

The boy ran through the dark woods. He could hear the man coming after him. The man shouted, "When I catch

you, I'm going to shoot you."

The boy ran on with the branches whipping him. Suddenly he found himself in the moonlight. He thought he'd entered a clearing, but it was narrow as a footpath. It was a deer run. He followed the deer run down a hill. He tried to walk quietly, as his father had taught him. He put his weight on one foot while he lifted the other, moved it forward, and placed it softly on the ground.

He could no longer hear the man behind him. As he moved silently the woods became still, and his heart quieted. He began to flow with the sounds in the woods—the wind, the soughing of the branches. He became calm.

The deer run angled steeply down the hill. He heard the sound of a stream somewhere before him. He continued on the path. The sound grew louder as he came to a high bank.

In the moonlight, he saw the stream flowing below him. The bank was ten feet high, too steep to climb down, and so he turned back. As he did, he heard a scolding jay. Something else was moving in the forest. The boy froze. He listened. He heard a twig snap. Someone was coming out of the woods toward the deer run.

As he watched, the branches parted some twenty feet from him. A shape moved onto the path, and the moonlight glinted on two bright dots in the forest. The moon slipped behind a cloud, and when it returned, the boy saw that the dots were the eyes of a bear.

He stood looking at the bear. The bear felt his presence and turned its head. The bear locked eyes with the boy and began to move toward him. The boy knew he should flee, but he could not move. He tried to move but he could not. The bear came closer. The boy began to shiver. He still could not move. The bear raised up on its hind feet. It was within five feet of the boy. The bear lifted its front legs, and a low growl came out of its throat.

The boy could smell the bear's breath and fur. The bear raised one paw and started to bring it down. Something flew across the boy's face. He heard an owl screech. He stepped back as the owl flew in his face. The step took him off of the tall bank, and the last thing he saw before he hit the water was the owl.

Steven was very cold. His clothes were wet. Something was prodding him in the back. He put his hand behind him, and he felt it was a nail protruding out of a fence post. His back was leaning up against a fencepost. He opened his eyes.

The sun was coming up. The boy was leaning against the post which held his mailbox. He was by the road leading to his house. He saw his house.

He got up slowly. His joints were all stiff and every part of him ached.

He looked up. His father was standing above him.

"Where have you been?" his father said.

They looked at each other.

"Where have you been?"

"I have *been* . . . , the boy said, "I have been after my ducks."

"I ordered you to go inside," the man said. "I told you to do that."

"Yes, you did," the boy said. "Yes, you did. And you told me that the ducks were mine. You said they were mine."

"They *were* yours," the man said. "I gave you the money for them. Now you go inside. You wash up, we have things to do."

The man walked away. Steven hung his head in shame. He sighed and started to the house.

"NO," he said, "no." His father turned. "They *were* mine," Steven said. "They *were* mine, you gave them to me. And I will not apologize. You took what was mine. You were wrong."

He followed his father to the barn. "You were *wrong*,"

he said. "I built this for them." And he took his father to the back of the barn and showed him the pen.

His father looked down at the pen.

"You were wrong," the boy said. "You were wrong to do what you did."

The man looked at his son a long time. He looked at the pen and back at the boy.

"I was wrong," he said. "I want you to forgive me." Steven nodded.

The two of them started out of the barn toward the house.

"I didn't do it to hurt you," the man said. The boy nodded. "That's a good pen you built. Next year we'll get you some more birds."

"Thank you," the boy said.

"And now I think you'd better get out of those wet clothes."

Steven went into the house. He dropped his jacket by the door and climbed the stairs to his room. He shed his wet clothes on the floor and turned on the hot water in the tub.

He laid out clean clothes on the bed. He glanced up at the calendar, at this month's picture of the ducks. The month was over. The boy reached up and pulled the old month's picture off. Underneath it was the new month and a picture of an owl.

THE END

ABOUT THE AUTHORS

DAVID MAMET is one of America's finest living playwrights. Among his best-known works are *American Buffalo,* and his *Glengarry Glen Ross* won the Pulitzer Prize and the New York Critics Circle Award as Best American Play of 1984. His most recent book is *Writing in Restaurants.*

LINDSAY CROUSE is an actress whose film credits include *The Trial* and *The Iceman.* She and her husband, Mr. Mamet, currently live in Cambridge, Massachusetts with their daughter.

ABOUT THE ARTIST

STEPHEN ALCORN is a young painter/printmaker who, while born in the United States, spent a large part of his childhood in Florence, Italy, which had a lasting influence on him. He began studying art as a young boy in Florence at the Istituto Statale d'Arte. He now works in a variety of media ranging from tempera to lithography, etching, woodcut and linoleum block printing. Stephen Alcorn has worked for major publishers in Europe and America. He, his wife Sabina, and their daughter Lucrezia now live and work in a large old house in Cambridge, New York.